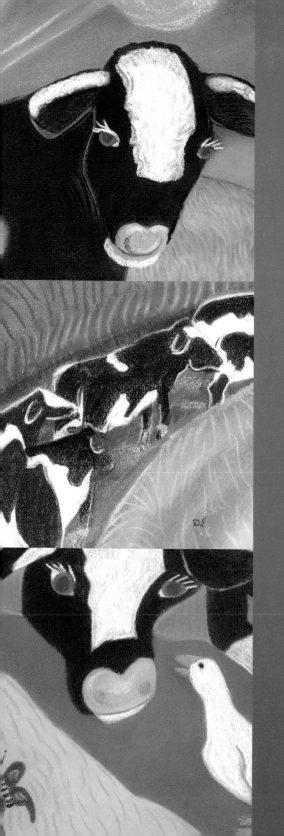

Moozie the cow loves children. She travels the country spreading the milk of human kindness as she presents programs for children at schools, churches and hospitals. Her mission is to teach children to be kind. She wants children to care for each other and not litter their minds with violence seen on TV, movies and video games.

Moozie is no ordinary cow; she is a full-size mechanical cow who emerged after many hours of Ted Dreier's puttering in the garage. She took on a life of her own with her first appearance at a Head Start School in Denton, Texas on March 11, 1998. It was immediately obvious that children loved Moozie. They wanted to touch her, pet her, talk to her. Since then Moozie has talked to thousands of children. Her mission continues to grow, and includes the establishment of Moozie's Kindness Foundation.

It is hoped the day will come when children see a cow, they will be reminded of the importance of kindness and accepting others.

Jane Morton was born and raised in Colorado where her family owned and operated a cattle ranch near Fort Morgan, Colorado. She's been writing for children for over twenty years. Her ten published books include middle grade novels as well as picture books in verse.

Jane Royse is a working artist living with three children on the shores of Lake Lewisville, Highland Village, Texas. Her childhood dream was to write and illustrate children's books; a dream given fruit from hours of reading to her children.

Ted Dreier grew up on a dairy farm in Kansas. The popularity of Moozie and the children's love of her has been his impetus to step back from 30 years in the corporate world as a public speaker and commit this chapter of his life to helping children understand the value of kindness and respect.

www.moozie.com

Moozie's Kind Adventure

Text Copyright © 1999 by Jane Morton
Illustration Copyright © 1999 by Jane Royse
Assistance by Moozie and Ted Dreier

Printed in Singapore

Published by Best Friends Books.
Library of Congress Catalog-in-Publication
Number 99-90526
ISBN 0-9662268-1-X
This book is threadsewn to last
until the cows come home.

This book may be ordered from the publisher.
Please include $3.50 for postage
and handling per book.
Always try your book store first.

Best Friends Books • 1-888-666-7155
P.O. Box 3880, Breckenridge, CO 80424

books@moozie.com
www.moozie.com

moozie's Kind Adventure

By Jane Morton   Assisted by Ted Dreier and Moozie   Illustrated by Jane Royse

Best Friends Books • Dallas, TX Breckenridge, CO • www.moozie.com

Big Moozie the cow is as kind as can be.
Not one other creature is kinder than she.

She stands gently flicking the flies with her tail,
While watching three ducklings at play near the trail.

She hears something coming and pricks up her ears.

Now what is this drum-drumming sound that she hears?

The hoofbeats of cattle. The herd's on the go.

It's heading her way to the valley below.

The cattle smell water and pick up their speed.

A fast-moving trot soon becomes a *stampede*.

If Moozie can't get the whole
herd turned around,
They'll trample the ducklings
right into the ground.

She tries shooing
ducklings back out of the way,
But they still continue to
frolic and play.

She tries moving closer
to shelter the three.
They will not be sheltered.
They'd rather run free.

"There's nobody else,
so it's all up to me.
I must turn the herd.
I will do it," says she.

The herd coming closer
is churning up dust.
"I can turn the herd.
Yes, I'll do it. I must."

She takes in some air and still more air and soon
Big Moozie swells up like a hot air balloon.

And just when it looks
as if Moozie might burst,
A small sound escapes
her, an uummmm sound
at first.

She draws on the air that
she's stored deep inside,
To send forth a Moooo
that will reach the divide.

Her MooooooOOO
gathers strength as it
booms off the hill.
She bellows so hard the
herd stops and stands still.

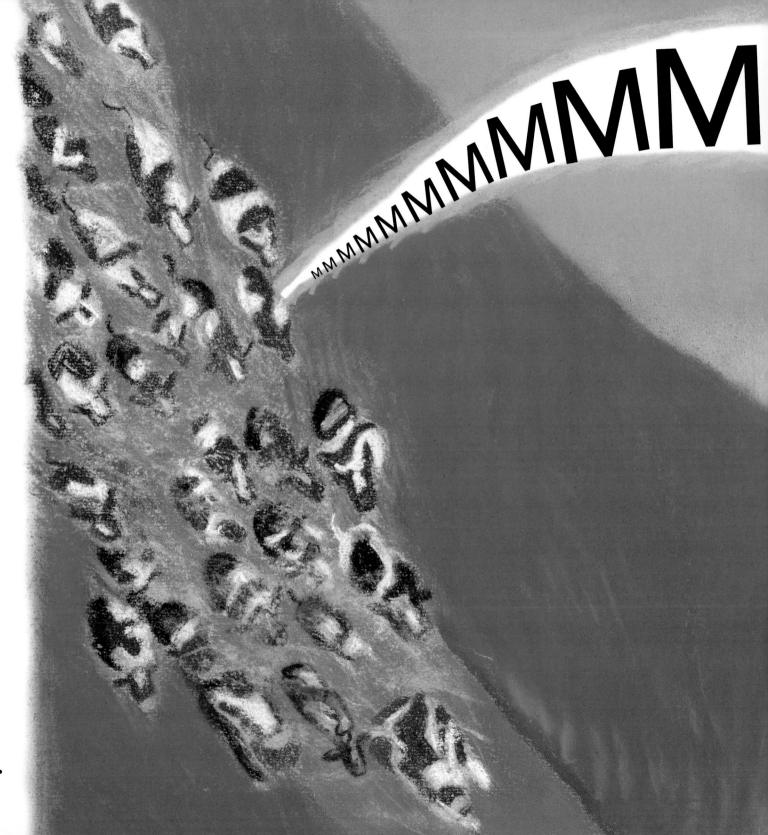

Loud echoes like thunder
fill cattle with fear.
The herd whirls around,
every heifer and steer.

They veer off toward water upon a new path,
While three little ducklings get on with their bath.

The mother duck
quacks, "Thanks
for saving my crew.
Not one other
creature is kinder
than you."

"I'm only one cow.
It was all up to me.
I did turn the herd,
and you're welcome,"
says she.

Moozie Books written by Ted Dreier

**Moozie's Cow Wisdom
For Life's Little Beefs**
First in a series of 96 page
mini-gift books filled with
original, humorous bits of
adult wisdom.
ISBN 0-9662268-0-1

**Moozie's Cow Wisdom for
Grabbing Life By The Horns**
The second in the series.
Bits of original wisdom
from a cow's perspective
for being all you can be.
ISBN 0-9662268-2-8

Moozie's Kindness Foundation

This non-profit foundation
focuses on reducing violence
among children by teaching
them the value of kindness at
a young age. With Moozie the
cow as the carrier of the message,
Ted Dreier presents educational
programs to children's forums.
This foundation has a growing
scope of activities.
If you would like to explore how
you might be a part of this mission,
please contact Ted Dreier, President
of Moozie's Kindness Foundation.

Email: Ted@moozie.com
1-800-699-4541

www.moozie.com

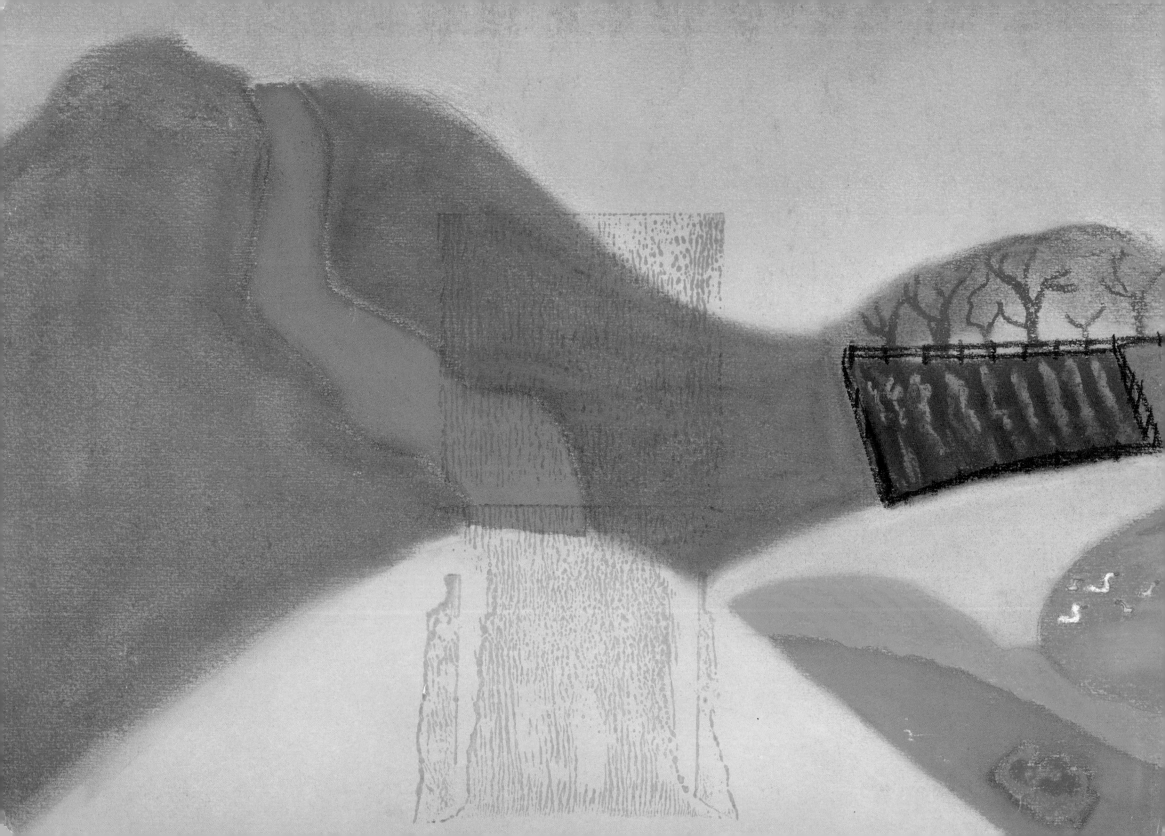